SpongeBob SquarePants®

BEHOLD, NO CAVITIES!
A Visit to the Dentist

by Sarah Willson illustrated by Harry Moore

SCHOLASTIC INC.
New York Toronto London Auckland Sydney
Mexico City New Delhi Hong Kong Buenos Aires

Stephen Hillenburg

Based on the TV series *SpongeBob SquarePants*® created by Stephen Hillenburg as seen on Nickelodeon®

ISBN-13: 978-0-545-00814-3
ISBN-10: 0-545-00814-X

12 11 10 9 8 7 6 5 4 3 2 1   8 9 10 11 12 13/0

Printed in the U.S.A.

First Scholastic printing, January 2008

"Today is the day! It's finally here!" said SpongeBob as he bounded out
of bed one morning.

"Meow!" said Gary.

"That's right, Gary. It *has* been exactly six months, two hours, and
seven minutes since my last dental cleaning. So today I get to go again!"

SpongeBob raced off to brush his teeth extra carefully.

Patrick came to visit while SpongeBob was still brushing.
"SpongeBob! What's wrong? You're foaming at the mouth!" he cried in alarm.

"Ish jusht tooshpashte, shilly," said SpongeBob, spitting out the toothpaste and showing Patrick his dazzling smile. "I flossed and now I'm brushing with my favorite toothbrush, just as I do each morning and night."

"Oh! I always wondered what that thing was," said Patrick, pointing at SpongeBob's toothbrush.

SpongeBob's mouth dropped open. "You don't floss or brush your teeth, Patrick?"

"Nope."

"Or . . . have semi-annual dental exams?"

"Nuh-uh."

"Have you *ever* been to a dentist?"

"What's a dentist?"

"Patrick, ol' buddy," he said when he had found his voice. "I think you had better come along with me to see my dentist, Dr. Gill, today. I'll call and make an appointment for you."

"Will it be scary?" Patrick asked, clutching onto SpongeBob outside the dentist's office.

SpongeBob smiled. "No, Patrick. Dr. Gill's office is the friendliest place in the world. And what's more, I am their favorite patient. Everyone here knows me! Just watch." He threw open the door.

"Hello! And who are you, young man?" asked the receptionist.
"I thought everyone here knew you," whispered Patrick.
"She must be new," SpongeBob whispered back.

"SpongeBob! You're here!" shrieked a voice.

"Hi, Debbie!" called SpongeBob. "Debbie is Dr. Gill's hygienist," he told Patrick. "She's the person who cleans your teeth."

"Do I hear SpongeBob?" called another voice.

"Hi, Dr. Gill!" said SpongeBob. "Dr. Gill makes sure you don't have any cavities, but if you do he'll fix them."

Just then Debbie and Dr. Gill burst into the waiting room. They joined
hands with SpongeBob and sang their favorite song:
  "I brush and floss my teeth each day
  To ward away that tooth decay!"

"Gee," said Patrick. "I had no idea getting your teeth cleaned could be this fun."

"Oh, Patrick," said SpongeBob, "you haven't seen *anything* yet!" He pulled Patrick into a hallway and pointed. "Behold! The No Cavi-Tree!"

"Wow. Why is it full of teeth that say 'SpongeBob'?" asked Patrick.
"Because you get your name posted up there when you have no cavities
at your checkup!" SpongeBob replied. "I get a new tooth every time I come
because I have never had a cavity."

"Time for your cleaning, SpongeBob!" called Debbie cheerfully. "First let's take a new X-ray."

Next Debbie cleaned SpongeBob's teeth. Then she polished his teeth with the bubble-gum-flavored tooth polish he chose, rinsed his teeth, and suctioned the water out of his mouth with Mr. Thirsty.

SpongeBob giggled. "That Mr. Thirsty always tickles!"

Then Dr. Gill had a look. "Your teeth look very healthy," he said. "We won't know for sure until we see the X-rays, but you certainly are a model dental patient!"

"Thanks, Dr. Gill," said SpongeBob. "Now it's time for you to look at my friend Patrick's teeth. He's never been to the dentist before."

Patrick got in the chair and opened his mouth. Debbie and Dr. Gill took turns peering in. Dr. Gill buzzed the receptionist. "Cancel the rest of the appointments today," he said. "This will take awhile."

Some hours LATER . . .

Finally Patrick's teeth were clean. "You can each go pick out a brand-new toothbrush now," Debbie said.

"Follow me, Patrick! I can't wait to see what colors they have!" cried SpongeBob.

"Oh, boys," called Dr. Gill. "I just learned that the light box we use to view your X-rays needs a new bulb. Why don't you go home and I'll call you both tomorrow with the results of your X-rays? By then the box will be fixed."

The next morning Patrick burst into SpongeBob's house. "No cavities!" he yelled. "Dr. Gill's receptionist called and told me! I get to have my name on the No Cavi-Tree!"

"Patrick! That's great!" said SpongeBob.

BRIIIING!

SpongeBob answered his phone. "Yes, this is SpongeBob. I . . . I . . .
what? Okay. I'll be there at two o'clock. Buh-buh-buh-bye." SpongeBob
hung up the phone and burst into tears. "I have four cavities!" he sobbed.

"I'll come with you to get them filled, old buddy," Patrick said, patting
his friend on the back.

That afternoon Patrick accompanied his friend to the dentist's office. SpongeBob's eyes welled up with fresh tears as they walked past the No Cavi-Tree.

"Hello again, SpongeBob and Patrick," said Dr. Gill. He looked at SpongeBob's X-rays. "It seems you have . . . wait. These aren't *your* X-rays!"

"They're not?" asked SpongeBob in a small voice.

"No! These are *Patrick's*! My new receptionist must have mixed them up!"

"I have no cavities?" said SpongeBob. "I HAVE NO CAVITIES!" he cried, leaping out of the chair with excitement.

"Woo-hoo! Way to go, SpongeBob!" shouted Patrick joyfully. Everyone linked arms and danced merrily. Suddenly a thought dawned on Patrick and he stopped dancing. "But that means *I* have cavities."

Debbie patted the chair. "Hop up, Patrick," she said kindly. "Dr. Gill will have these filled in a jiffy."